yellow-billed cuckoo

barn swallow
nest 5 inches across

magpie
nest 15 inches across

American f
nest 2$\frac{1}{2}$ fee

wren
nest 5 inches across

The Magpies' Nest

Retold by JOANNA FOSTER
Illustrated by JULIE DOWNING

CLARION BOOKS/*New York*

Clarion Books, a Houghton Mifflin Company imprint
215 Park Avenue South, New York, NY 10003

Text copyright © 1995 by Joanna Foster
Illustrations copyright © 1995 by Julie Downing
Art executed in watercolor and colored pencil on 300 lb. Fabriano paper.
The text was set in 16/19 pt. Centaur.

Printed in the USA

Library of Congress Cataloging-in-Publication Data
Foster, Joanna.
The Magpies' nest / retold by Joanna Foster ; illustrated by Julie Downing.
p. cm.
Summary: A story, based on English folklore, explains why each bird
builds its nest in a different way.
ISBN 0-395-62155-0
[1. Birds—Nests—Folklore. 2. Nest building—Folklore. 3. Animals—Habitations
—Folklore. 4. England—Folklore.] I. Downing, Julie, ill. II. Title.
PZ8.1.F8144Mag 1995
398.24'528864—dc20
[E] 94-1773
CIP
AC

WOZ 10 9 8 7 6 5 4 3 2 1

~ For Barbara Reed ~

*who knows the heart of storytelling
and shares it so generously*
—J. F.

~ to Ellen ~

—J. D.

Once upon a time in the spring of the world, the air was full of the sound of birds, twittering, singing, chirping, and calling, "Time to lay eggs. Time to lay eggs."

But if you listened closely you could hear that the birds were also arguing.

"Where shall we put the eggs?" chirped the robin.

"Any old place. Any old place," cried the gulls. "Put them on the rocks or in the reeds."

"No, no," squawked the bluejay. "My eggs are too precious for that. I need some kind of small, safe place."

"Yes," whistled the swans, "a nest. A nest is what we want."

Other birds picked that up. "Nests, nests. We need nests. We need nests."

"But wait," said the robin. "What is a nest, and how do you build one?"

All the birds fell silent.

Then two black birds with bold white markings and long iridescent tails circled up from a thorn tree. These were Mother and Father Magpie. Loudly they called, "We can show you, we can show you. Watch us. We magpies know how to build a nest."

The birds all flew to the thorn tree and eagerly gathered around the magpies. All, that is, except the whippoorwill, who was nestled in the leaves on the ground. "I'm so comfortable," she said to herself. "I'm sure I can see enough from here."

"We start with mud," announced Father Magpie. He and Mother Magpie set off for a nearby river and returned with dabs of mud in their beaks. Back and forth they flew.

"Make it of mud," honked the flamingo. "That's easy enough." Spreading her great wings and stretching her long legs out behind her, she flew away.

To this day, flamingoes make their nests only of mud.

"Dabs of mud, dabs of mud," twittered the swallow. "I see. I see how it's done." And she, too, swooped off.

Swallows are still building their nests with dabs of mud.

Next the magpies flew into the woods, calling back, "Sticks, sticks. You also need sticks for a nest." One by one they brought back sticks and arranged them around the mud.

"That's it," decided the eagle. "I'll make a nest of stout sticks and branches." And the eagle flew away screaming, "Sticks, sticks, sticks."

"Sticks and twigs," sang the little house wren. "Tiny, tiny sticks and twigs. I see how it's done." Flicking her tail, she flitted away in search of a cozy place to start her nest building.

"Wait, wait," called Mother Magpie. "There is more to it. We're not finished." But by this time, the flamingo and swallow, the eagle and wren were long gone.

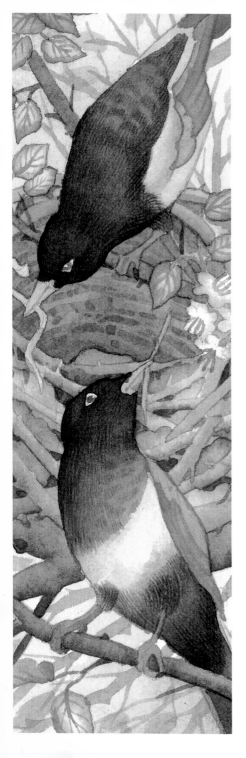

"Now, you must also weave in grasses and twigs," said Father Magpie. He and Mother Magpie began poking a twig in here and a blade of grass in there.

"So, the real secret of nest building is weaving!" trilled the oriole. "I'm very good at that." As she flew away she thought, "I can do much better than the magpies. My nest will hang down from the branch rather than perching on top."

By now, a number of the birds had left. But the cuckoo and the cowbird, who were always late, had just arrived. They crowded in to take a closer look, and asked, "What's going on? What is that?"

"This is a nest," Father Magpie answered impatiently. "We are showing you how to build a nest."

"It looks like a lot of work," complained the cuckoo.

Mother Magpie arrived with some thistledown and began to line the nest. Father Magpie flew off and came back with a long hair from a horse's tail. "And we'll soon have moss and string and paper and even the skin from a snake," he sang with delight.

"Horsehair is good," chirped the sparrows, and a flock of them rose in the air and left.

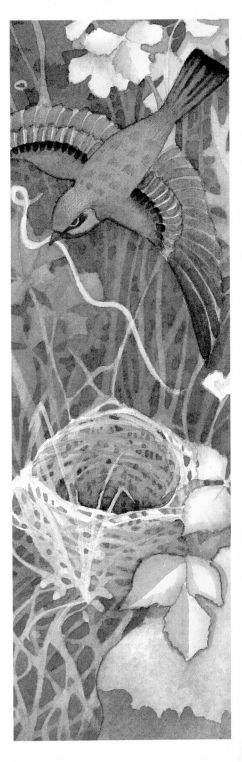

"Moss and perhaps some spiderweb might be all I really need," mused the hummingbird, and this tiniest of the birds whirred away with the others.

Watching them go, the cowbird said to the cuckoo, "You know, I'd like to have my eggs in a nest like that, but I wouldn't want to do all that work."

"Maybe we don't have to do the work," the cuckoo said slyly. "Why not just let the others do it?"

"Why not indeed!" agreed the cowbird, and they flew away. To this day, cowbirds and cuckoos always sneak their eggs into the nests of other birds.

The magpies were busier than ever. After lining the nest, they built a dome over it woven of twigs and sticks and grasses. Finally their nest was finished. But when they looked around for their audience, all the birds had gone.

All except the whippoorwill, nestled in the leaves on the ground. The magpies flew down beside her.

"Now do you see how a nest is built?" asked Father Magpie proudly.

"Thank you. It's lovely," replied the whippoorwill. She did not want to seem ungrateful, but in fact she had been asleep the whole time.

As the magpies flew back to their nest, she sighed and said to herself, "No matter. These leaves would make a pleasant nest. I'll just hide my eggs here."

This, then, is how it came about that no two kinds of birds make their nests in the same way.

Author's Note

Joseph Jacobs told the story "Magpie's Nest" in his book *English Fairy Tales*, which was published in the late 1890s. In the afterword he wrote that he built his story on two "myths" that he had found "in the Reverend Mr. Swainson's *Folklore of British Birds.*"

What part of Britain did this tale come from? How old is it? We do not know. Much of British folklore has roots that are centuries old. Before printed books were known in England, stories and sayings were passed on by word of mouth. With the advent of printing, John Aubrey wrote in the late 1600s, "the many good Bookes putt all the old Fables out of doors." For a while the oral tradition continued among country people, but during the Industrial Revolution, when many of the country people moved into the cities, the old folkways were discarded and began to disappear. Following the example of Wilhelm and Jakob Grimm in Germany, the English became interested in preserving their own folklore. The Folk-Lore Society was founded in 1878, and people like the Rev. Mr. Swainson traveled through the countryside, collecting the tales that people still remembered.

I first encountered the magpie and her impatient friends when I read Jacobs as a child. I have thought of them often over the years, especially when I found myself wanting to leave a lecture or concert before the end.

In retelling the story, I sought information about birds and their habits, as did Joseph Jacobs. Jacobs acknowledged the help he got "from a little friend of mine named Katie." My help came from books and magazine articles. Perhaps my most interesting discovery was that while the nests of many species are built by either the female or the male, some nests are built by both birds working together. Among the birds that work together in pairs are the magpies. So while in Jacobs' story the skillful builder is "Madge Magpie" alone, I thought my version should include her mate as well.

A final word about magpies, fascinating members of the crow family. They are gregarious birds with a reputation for predicting things to come. Some say they are harbingers of good fortune, others that they are omens of bad luck. This ancient rhyme from Lancashire, England, tells what to expect when you see a certain number of magpies:

> *One for sorrow,*
> *Two for mirth,*
> *Three for a wedding,*
> *Four for a birth,*
> *Five for rich,*
> *Six for poor,*
> *Seven for a witch,*
> *I can tell you no more.*

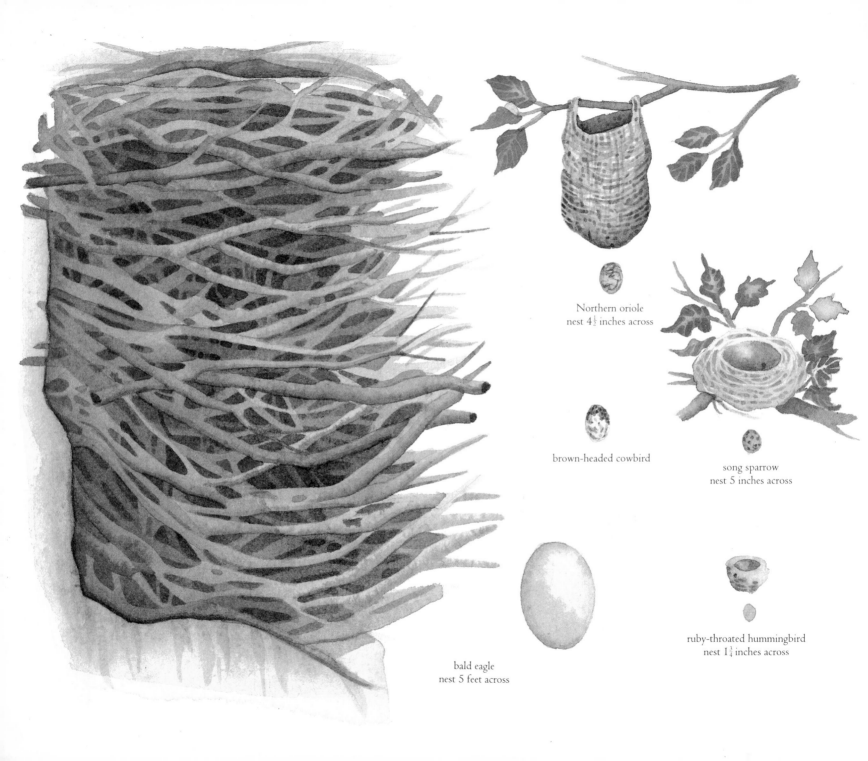

Northern oriole
nest 4½ inches across

brown-headed cowbird

song sparrow
nest 5 inches across

ruby-throated hummingbird
nest 1¾ inches across

bald eagle
nest 5 feet across